Ashley Small & ASHLEE TALL

The GRASS is ALWAYS GREENER

by Michele Jakubowski

illustrated by Neil

PICTURE WINDOW BOOKS
a capstone imprint

Ashley Small and Ashlee Tall is published by Picture Window Books.
A Capstone Imprint
1710 Roe Crest Drive
North Mankato, Minnesota 56003
www.mycapstone.com

Library of Congress Cataloging-in-Publication Data
Names: Jakubowski, Michele, author.
Title: The grass is always greener / by Michele Jakubowski.
Description: North Mankato, Minnesota : Picture Window Books, an imprint of
Capstone Press, [2017] | Series: Ashley Small and Ashlee Tall |
Summary: Ashley has a baby brother Sam who is cute because he is just beginning
to talk, but is also cranky because his teeth are erupting; Ashlee has a twelve-year-old
sister who can be fun, but also often ignores her younger sister—so the
eight-year-old friends cannot decide which of them has a worse sibling situation.
Identifiers: LCCN 2016003609| ISBN 9781515800125 (library binding) |
ISBN 9781515800163 (pbk.) | ISBN 9781515800200 (ebook pdf)
Subjects: LCSH: Best friends—Juvenile fiction. | Brothers and sisters—Juvenile fiction.
| Families—Juvenile fiction. | CYAC: Best friends—Fiction. |
Friendship—Fiction. | Brothers and sisters—Fiction. | Family life—Fiction.
Classification: LCC PZ7.J153556 Gr 2017 | DDC 813.6—dc23
LC record available at http://lccn.loc.gov/2016003609

Design by Lori Bye

Printed in Canada.
009713F16

Table of contents

2353

Ash

Ashley "Ash" Sanchez may be small, but she's mighty! Ash likes to play all types of games — from sports to video games — and she loves to win. Ash may be loud and silly, but more than anything, she is a great friend!

Lee

Ashlee Taylor, otherwise known as Lee, is tall and graceful. When Lee is not twirling around in her dance classes, she can be found drawing or painting. Lee may be shy around new people, but she is as sweet and as kind as could be!

chapter one

{ BABY BROTHER }

"I love birthday parties!" exclaimed eight-year-old Ashley Sanchez.

"Me too!" replied her best friend, Ashlee Taylor. "I can't wait for the birthday cake!"

Ashley, or Ash as her friends called her, and Ashlee, otherwise known as Lee, may have been best friends, but they were different in almost every way.

While Lee was looking forward to the sweet, sugary birthday cake, Ash wasn't interested. Instead, she was wondering if there was any leftover pizza. Another difference was their size. Ash was small, while Lee was tall. Some people even called them Ashley Small and Ashlee Tall!

As different as the girls were, they were both having a great time at the first birthday party of Ash's brother, Sam. Ash's parents had invited all of their friends, including Lee and her family.

The person having the most fun, though, was the birthday boy.

Sam was grinning and clapping his chubby little hands. He was sitting in his high chair waiting for his birthday cake. Ash and Lee sat on either side of him.

"Is that a new tooth?" Lee asked as she pointed into Sam's mouth.

"Yep, it popped through this week," Ash told her. "But be careful. He bit my finger and it hurt!"

Lee had never paid much attention to Sam before. When he was first born, all he did was eat and sleep.

"He is so cute!" Lee said. "Does he talk yet?"

Ash's eyes widened with excitement. "He just started! Watch this!"

Ash turned to get Sam's attention. "Hey, Sam! Say 'Ashley,'" she told him.

Sam smiled and giggled. Ash tried again. "Say, 'Ashley.'"

It took Ash a few more tries, but Sam finally said, "Ashy!"

Lee clapped her hands and said, "That is awesome! Do you think he can say 'Lee'?"

"I don't know," Ash said. "Let's see."

Ash turned toward Sam again. When she had his attention she asked, "Sam, can you say 'Lee'?"

Sam tilted his head. He was unsure what she was asking. He put his finger in his mouth and didn't say a word.

Ash pointed at Lee and tried again. "This is Lee. Can you say her name? Lee!"

This time Sam smiled. He took his finger out of his mouth. He pointed it at Lee. "Lee-Lee!" he giggled.

"He said my name!" Lee cheered.

Ash laughed. "He sure did!"

"What else can he do?" Lee asked. She never knew babies could be so much fun!

Ash thought for a moment. "I don't know. Normal baby stuff," she said with a shrug. Then she remembered something. "Oh! He did just start dancing. It's so funny! When my dad plays his guitar, Sam bounces up and down. Sometimes he gets so excited he falls over!"

Lee laughed as she thought about Sam dancing and falling over.

Just then, Mrs. Sanchez came into the room. She was carrying a huge birthday cake with a single candle. Everyone started singing to Sam. He was so happy! He began twisting around in his chair and reaching out for the cake.

Mrs. Sanchez set the cake on the table in front of him. She thought it was out of his reach but Sam stretched out his arm as far as he could. He grabbed a chunk out of the side and shoved the entire fistful of cake into his mouth. Then Sam smiled a huge, messy grin. Everyone laughed and cheered. Sam loved the attention! He clapped his frosting-covered hands and laughed.

Lee leaned over to Ash and said, "You are so lucky to have a baby brother!"

chapter two

{ BIG SISTER }

After Lee had finished her cake and Ash had eaten another slice of pizza, the girls decided to take a break from the birthday party. They went to Ash's room to hang out for a bit.

"What should we do?" Lee asked. "Want to draw?"

"Nah," Ash replied. "Want to play a game?"

Lee shook her head. "Not really."

As they tried to think of something to do, Lee's older sister, Mallory, walked into Ash's room. Mallory was twelve years old. She didn't usually spend much time with Ash and Lee.

"What are you two doing?" Mallory asked.

"Nothing yet," Lee told her. "We can't think of anything."

Mallory looked around Ash's room. She walked over to the bookshelf and picked up a box.

"What's this?" she asked Ash.

"That's the makeup I used last Halloween for my zombie costume," Ash replied. "I looked super creepy!"

Mallory opened the box and looked at the brushes and makeup. Suddenly, she had an idea. "Hey, do you two want to do silly makeovers?"

"What's a silly makeover?" Ash said.

"We can use this makeup on each other, but instead of trying to look nice, we can see who can look the silliest," Mallory explained.

"Sure, why not?" Lee said.

"Sounds fun!" Ash added.

Mallory had the most experience with makeup, so the girls decided that she would do Ash's makeover. Ash sat on the floor across from Mallory. As she worked, Mallory told them funny stories about her friends and the fun things they did together.

They all giggled and had a great time. Ash didn't know anyone Mallory's age. Her stories were so interesting to Ash!

When she was finished, Mallory asked, "Are you ready to see yourself?"

Ash nodded as Mallory held up a mirror. She didn't know what to expect.

"Ahh!" Ash screamed with surprise. "I look like an evil clown!"

"I told you it would look funny!" Mallory said.

All three of them burst out laughing.

"You better not let our mom see you!" Lee said.

"No kidding!" Mallory said, and laughed even harder.

Ash didn't understand. "Why can't your mom see me?"

Lee tried to stop laughing so she could explain, but she couldn't. Every time she and Mallory looked at each other, they laughed even harder. Ash wanted to understand the joke so she could join in the fun.

Finally, Lee caught her breath and explained. "For some reason, our mom is afraid of clowns."

Mallory turned toward Lee and asked, "Remember that Halloween when she had to stop answering the door because there were so many clown costumes?"

"Yes!" Lee replied. She and Mallory started laughing all over again. Lee was laughing so hard there were tears in her eyes. "She was even afraid of little kids!"

As Ash watched Lee and Mallory having such a great time, she thought, *Lee is so lucky to have a big sister!*

chapter three

{ THE LUCKY ONE }

A few days after Sam's birthday party, Ash and Lee were playing in Lee's backyard. They were practicing their cartwheels.

Lee kicked her long legs over gracefully. She did three cartwheels in a row. When she was done, she giggled. All that spinning had made her feel a little dizzy.

Cartwheels had been harder for Ash to learn. She was determined to do them right. She kept trying and was finally able to kick her legs all the way over.

"I did it!" she shouted.

"Way to go!" Lee cheered.

The pair decided to take a break and went to relax in the yard.

"Sam's birthday party was so much fun," Lee said as she stretched out on a lawn chair.

"It was," Ash agreed. She sat back, closed her eyes, and enjoyed feeling the warm sun on her face.

"I wish I had a baby brother," said Lee, giving a sigh.

Ash's eyes popped open. "What?" she said. "Why would you want a baby brother?"

"Sam is so cute!" Lee told her. "It was so much fun to play with him at his birthday party. Remember when he said my name?"

Ash nodded. "Yes, but it's not fun when he wakes up crying in the middle of the night. Usually he cries for my mom and dad. Last night he started yelling 'Ashy! Ashy!' I thought he would never go back to sleep."

Lee giggled. "You are so lucky! If I had a baby brother that woke up in the middle of the night, I would go into his room and play with him until he went back to sleep. It would be great!"

"It's not that easy. Believe me," Ash said. She rolled her eyes. "Besides, you're the lucky one. I'd much rather have an older sister. Mallory does so many fun things with you!"

Lee shook her head. "The only reason Mallory hung out with us at Sam's party was because she was bored. All of the other kids there were babies. Usually the only thing she says to me is, 'Get out of my room!' or 'Don't touch my stuff!' And she doesn't let me hang out with her when her friends are around. Trust me, a baby brother is way better than a big sister."

Ash wasn't convinced. "Mallory is so much fun. Plus, you two have all those silly stories you share. I can't do that with Sam. He can barely talk."

Just then, Mrs. Taylor called the girls in for lunch. As they headed inside, Ash and Lee were both certain that the other was the lucky one.

chapter four

{ THE MALL }

Mrs. Taylor loved it when Ash ate at their house. She knew that Lee would only eat a plain cheese sandwich with the crusts cut off and a sliced apple. Ash, on the other hand, would try anything.

"I picked up some meats and cheeses from the deli to make Italian subs. I also picked a tomato from the garden. How does that sound?" Mrs. Taylor asked Ash.

"Sounds great to me!" Ash smiled.

When the girls had finished their lunches, Mrs. Taylor told Lee they needed to go to the mall to pick out new shoes.

Lee knew Ash didn't like shopping, but she asked her anyway. "Want to go with us?"

Ash shook her head. "No, thanks."

"Can we go later?" Lee asked her mom. While Lee loved shopping, she wanted to play more with Ash.

"I'm sorry, honey, but we need to go now," Mrs. Taylor responded. "I told Mallory she could meet some friends at the mall at one o'clock."

Ash sat up. "Actually, I'll go," she said.

Lee looked at her friend with confusion. "You will?"

"Sure," Ash shrugged. "Why not?"

***

As they drove to the mall, Mallory sat in the front seat next to Mrs. Taylor. Ash and Lee sat behind them. Ash had loved spending time with Mallory at Sam's party. She was happy to be hanging out with her again.

Ash leaned forward. She whispered to Mallory, "I sure hope there aren't any clowns at the mall!"

Mallory turned around. She frowned and asked, "What?"

Ash giggled and nodded her head toward Mrs. Taylor. She whispered, "You know — clowns! Remember?"

"Oh yeah," Mallory said with a little smile. She turned back around and started playing with the car radio. Before Ash could say anything else, Mallory found a song she liked and turned up the volume.

Ash sat back. She looked over at Lee who was smiling and shaking her head.

***

Mallory's friends were waiting for her at the entrance of the mall. Mallory ran toward them. They all giggled and hugged each other. Ash ran up behind Mallory, dragging Lee along with her.

"Let's go check out that new lip gloss," one of Mallory's friends said.

"Good idea!" Ash said. She turned toward Mallory and said, "We can use it when we do silly makeovers!"

Mallory and her friends went silent. They looked at Ash like she was an alien.

As Mrs. Taylor joined the group, Mallory whined to her, "Mom, you didn't say I had to watch the little girls at the mall!"

This made Ash feel terrible. Had Mallory just called her and Lee "little girls"? Ash was not a little girl!

"Ash and Lee will be shopping with me," Mrs. Taylor said. "We'll meet you back here at three."

As they walked away, Lee put her arm around Ash. Lee could tell that Ash was upset by what Mallory had said. "Come on," Lee said. "After we get shoes, I'll ask my mom if we can play at the arcade for a little bit."

chapter five

{ WHAT A MESS }

A few days after they had gone to the mall, Ash called Lee to see if she could play.

"Want to go to the park? Or ride our bikes?" Ash asked.

Lee thought for a minute. "Is Sam home?" she asked.

Ash laughed. "Of course he's home. He's a baby! Where else would he be?"

Lee giggled. "Actually, could I come over? We can teach Sam some new words and you can show me how he dances."

Ash didn't really feel like playing with her baby brother, but she knew Lee wasn't going to give up.

"Okay, fine," she said. "We can play with Sam for a little bit and then we can go for a bike ride."

"Great!" Lee said. "I'll be over in ten minutes!"

As Lee rode her bicycle over to Ash's, she was excited about playing with Sam. She remembered how much fun she'd had playing with him at his birthday party.

When Lee got to Ash's apartment building, she raced up the stairs. Before she could knock, she heard crying coming from the other side of the door.

"What's wrong with Sam?" Lee asked as Ash opened the door.

Ash rolled her eyes. "He's getting more teeth. It's making him very upset."

"Poor guy!" Lee said as she walked in. "I bet I can cheer him up."

"Good luck," Ash mumbled.

Lee found Sam sitting on the living room floor. His face was red and wet with tears. He had one of his hands shoved into his mouth.

"Hey, buddy!" Lee knelt beside him.

Sam smiled without taking his hand out of his mouth. "Lee-Lee!" he said, although it was hard to understand him.

Lee laughed. As she got closer to Sam, she noticed thick snot was dripping from his nose. Lee did not like snotty noses!

"Oh!" she said as she sat back. "I think he needs a tissue!"

Ash grabbed a tissue and quickly wiped Sam's nose. "His nose runs a lot when he's getting new teeth," she said.

Sam didn't like having his nose wiped. He began crying again.

"Hey, little guy! Don't cry!" Lee told him. She handed Sam a toy block.

Sam put the block right into his mouth and began chewing on it. A second later he tried to give the block back to Lee, but now it was covered in drool.

"Um, no thanks," Lee said. She didn't want to touch the wet block.

Sam whined and wiggled around. He looked like he might burst into tears. Lee didn't want his nose to start running again.

Lee tried to pat Sam on the back. As she leaned toward him, though, she got a whiff of a horrible smell.

"Gross! What is that smell?" she gasped.

Ash laughed. "Didn't I tell you? He has extra yucky diapers when he's getting new teeth. I'll go get my mom."

As Ash left the room, Lee looked at Sam. He had been so sweet and adorable at his party. Now he seemed so messy and cranky. What had happened?

chapter six

{ ALMOST SISTERS }

By the time Ash and her mom returned to the living room, Sam was crying hard again. Lee was happy when Mrs. Sanchez scooped him up.

"Time for a new diaper and a nap," she said as they headed for Sam's room.

Lee got up from the floor and sat on the couch. Ash plopped down next to her. She could tell that Lee was sad.

"Sam's not always that grumpy," Ash said. "He can be a lot of fun, but not all of the time."

Lee smiled and nodded. She had been looking forward to playing with Sam.

Ash suddenly had an idea. "Hey! Once Sam gets his new teeth, he'll be in a better mood. Maybe then you can help me teach him how to ride the new scooter he got for his birthday."

Lee asked, "You mean the little red one that looks like a fire truck?"

"That's the one," Ash said. "We can teach him how to scoot with his legs and how to honk the horn."

"That sounds fun!" Lee liked the idea of helping Sam learn something new.

Just then Lee had a good idea of her own. "Are you free on Saturday? Do you want to go to the movies with Mallory and me? We're going to see the new Beach Dogs movie."

Ash loved the Beach Dogs movies! They were about dogs who talked with human voices and did all kinds of crazy things.

Ash started to say yes, but then she thought of something else. "Are Mallory's friends going?"

Ash did not like the way Mallory had acted around her friends.

Lee shook her head. "Nope. Mallory said none of her friends like Beach Dogs anymore, but she still does."

Ash remembered how Mallory called her and Lee "little girls."

"Do you think Mallory will want me to come?" Ash asked.

"Definitely," Lee said. "Mallory said that she thinks you are funny."

"She did?" Ash asked excitedly.

"Yep. After Sam's party she said she had a lot of fun doing silly makeovers with you," Lee said.

"We did have fun, didn't we?" Ash smiled.

"We did," Lee agreed. "I guess big sisters are like baby brothers. Sometimes they are fun, and sometimes they are cranky!"

Lee and Ash giggled.

"Too bad we aren't sisters," Ash said.

"We kind of are," Lee replied. "Best friends are like sisters you get to pick. That's what my mom always says."

Ash's eyes widened. "So that means Mallory is like my older sister and Sam is your little brother!"

"Yeah!" Lee laughed. "Since we're best friends, we get the best of both worlds!"

GLOSSARY

arcade (ahr-KADE) — a business with machines to play games, such as pinball

cartwheels (KAHRT-weels) — circular, sideways handsprings with arms and legs extended

confusion (kuhn-FYOO-zhuhn) — the state of being uncertain or puzzled about something

cranky (KRAN-kee) — acting in an annoyed way

diapers (DYE-purs) — pieces of soft clothing worn as underwear by babies and toddlers

dizzy (DIZ-ee) — having the feeling of spinning around and being unsteady on your feet

leftover (LEFT-oh-vur) — something that hasn't yet been used or eaten

makeover (MAKE-oh-vur) — an act of changing a person's appearance, usually with makeup, a new hairdo, or new clothes

relax (ri-LAKS) — to take a rest

whiff (WIF) — a faint smell in the air

whined (WINDE) — complained about something in an annoying way

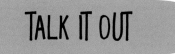

TALK IT OUT

1. Ash and Lee each get annoyed with their siblings once in a while. Do you have siblings? If so, have you ever wished for a different brother or sister? If not, have you ever wished you had one?

2. Why do you think Mallory was rude to Ash and Lee when she met her friends at the mall? Discuss the possibilities.

3. What is the theme of this story? How do you know?

WRITE IT DOWN

1. What characteristics does Ash have that are different from Lee? Write a paragraph describing how they are different.

2. Would you rather have Sam or Mallory as a sibling? Write a story or a poem that reflects your answer, using examples from the text.

3. Write a review of *The Grass Is Always Greener*. Include a short summary of the story, setting, and characters. Then write what you liked or didn't like about the book.

MAKE A FAMILY TREE

A family tree is a chart or drawing that shows how members of a family are related to one another. In this activity, you'll make your own family tree.

what you need

- Pencil
- Colored pencils
- Paper
- Scissors
- Glue

what you do

1. Use a pencil to draw the outline of a tree. Make it big, so that it takes up most of the page. After you've drawn the outline, fill in your tree with lots of branches.

2. Color in the tree trunk and branches with a brown colored pencil.

3. On a different sheet of paper, draw outlines of leaves. Make them big enough to include one or two sentences of writing.

4. Cut out your leaves, and write the name of one family member inside each leaf in a dark color. You can include anyone you think of as part of your family!

5. After you write the person's name, include one thing that you love about him or her. For example, Ash might write, "Sam Sanchez — I love that Sam is learning to talk!"

6. Once you've written inside all of the leaves, color them in lightly with a green pencil.

7. Paste your leaves onto the tree branches, and you've got your very own family tree!

ABOUT THE AUTHOR

Michele Jakubowski has the teachers in her life to thank for her love of reading and writing. While writing has always been a passion for Michele, she believes it is the books she has read throughout the years, and the teachers who assigned them, that have made her the storyteller she is today. Raised in the Chicago suburb of Hoffman Estates, Michele now lives in Powell, Ohio, with her husband, John, and their children, Jack and Mia.

ABOUT THE ILLUSTRATOR

Born in Transylvania, Hédi Fekete grew up watching and drawing her favorite cartoon characters. Each night, her mother read her beautiful bedtime stories, which made her love for storytelling grow. Hédi's love for books and animation stuck with her through the years, inspiring her to become an illustrator, digital artist, and animator.

THE FUN DOESN'T STOP HERE!

Discover more at *www.capstonekids.com*

Videos and Contests
Games and Puzzles
Friends and Favorites
Authors and Illustrators

Find cool websites and more books like this one
at *www.facthound.com*. Just type in the
Book ID: 9781515800125 and you're ready to go!